בס"ד

The Secret of
Carlos Romanus

by Esther Kosofsky

illustrations by Chana Min Hahar

Hachai
PUBLISHING

The Secret of Carlos Romanus

First Edition - Adar 5778 / March 2018

In memory of my beloved father
R. Dovid ben Yechezkal Meir HaLevi Edelman z"l. E. K.

Dedicated, with love, to my parents. C. M. H.

Editor: D. L. Rosenfeld
Layout: Moshe Cohen

ISBN-13: 978-1-945560-08-8
LCCN: 2017961171

HACHAI PUBLISHING
Brooklyn, N.Y.
Tel: 718-633-0100 Fax: 718-633-0103
www.hachai.com - info@hachai.com

Printed in China

Table of Contents

Author's Note

For so many people, Pesach (Passover) preparation includes hours of cleaning, searching and removing all chametz (leavened food) from the house before the next phase begins, shopping and cooking the wonderful foods that are served only on Pesach.

For my older siblings and me in the Edelman family of Springfield, MA, Pesach meant this and more. In our house, the primary focus before Pesach was helping our father, Rabbi Dovid HaLevi Edelman, z"l, bring specially-made, hand-baked matzot to people throughout the region. We vied for the right to prepare the matza in the proper boxes and to accompany our beloved father as he made his yearly rounds with matza in hand and a warm smile on his face.

As Pesach approached, we looked forward to another special event: my father's yearly rendition of Carlos Romanus. This story was an oral tradition that our father told every year during the lunch meals of Pesach. This tale was too exciting, too rich, too gripping to be contained in one sitting. It stretched out over many courses and kept the children – and later the grandchildren – at the edge of our seats, as our revered father magically wove the tale as only he could.

Time went on, and the family spread out all over the globe, no longer able to gather together for Pesach. That's when I committed to putting the saga of Carlos Romanus on paper to share with the new generation. Relying on memory that goes back to my early years, I attempted to tell the story as I recalled hearing it from my father. He read the first draft and approved.

I am grateful to Hachai Publishing for allowing me the opportunity to share the story of Carlos Romanus with you. I may have taken a little liberty with the story in its final form, but through it all, it remains a story of faith and the undeniable hand of Hashem (G-d) in our lives.

My father z"l passed away before seeing his story in book form, but I dedicate this book to him. May the memory of Dovid ben Yechezkal Meir HaLevi live on through all who read and enjoy *The Secret of Carlos Romanus.*

Esther (Edelman) Kosofsky

Meet the Characters

Moshe Levi

Moshe Levi is a brave and clever fifteen-year-old boy who lives in Amsterdam. He is determined to support his family after his father passes away.

Esther Levi

Esther Levi is a loving parent who worries about her son's business trip to faraway Africa.

Yosef Levi

Yosef Levi is only ten, but he has big opinions and wants to be treated like an adult.

Miriam Levi

Miriam Levi is three years old, a sweet little girl who misses Moshe when he's away.

Carlos Romanus

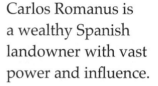

Carlos Romanus is a wealthy Spanish landowner with vast power and influence.

Bella Romanus

Bella Romanus is the wife of Carlos, mother of Diego and Rita.

Rita & Diego

Rita and Diego are the Romanus children, growing up in a wealthy, luxurious home.

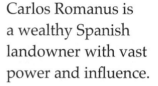

Manuel

Manuel is the trusted servant of Carlos Romanus who's known him since childhood.

Words in Other Languages

This Fun-to-Read adventure takes place in more than one location. Some characters live in Amsterdam, where people speak Dutch, while others live in Spain and speak Spanish. There are a few words from both languages used within the story.

Dutch

Meneer (Mih-neer) ....Mister

Dank je (Donk-yeh) ....Thank you

Spanish

Agua (Ag-wa) .... Water

Señor (Sen-yor) .... Mister

Señora (Sen-yo-ra) ....Mrs.

Gracias (Grah-see-yas) ....Thank you

Buenas noches (Bweh-nas noh-chess) .... Good night

In keeping with the setting of the story, the spelling of Hebrew words and phrases is consistent with Sephardic pronunciation.

Map of Amsterdam's Jewish Community

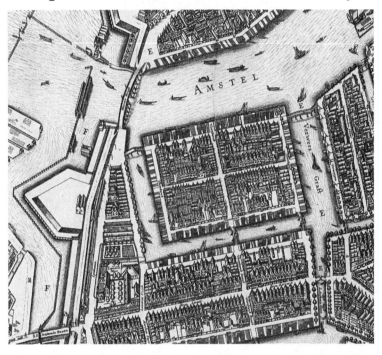

Vlooienburg, also known as Vloonburch, was the location of Amsterdam's art market and lumber trade. It was also the center of Amsterdam's Jewish community. By 1639, there were over a thousand Jewish residents living peacefully among their Dutch neighbors, free to observe Judaism quietly and in private, without interference from local authorities.

Chapter One
The Journey

Moshe Levi jumped off the wagon before it stopped moving. He swung his heavy pack onto his back and took a deep breath of the salty sea air. There she was! The ship he was to board here in Amsterdam stood with sails unfurled, ready to depart for the faraway continent of Africa.

The sturdy fifteen-year-old couldn't have been more excited. Finally, he had the chance to be a man, to earn money for Mama and the children now that Papa was gone.

Moshe held out his hand to help Mama down from the wagon. How pale she looked in her black gown and shawl.

"Don't worry, Mama," he said, for the tenth time that day. "I must travel to buy goods, just like Papa did, and then we will have as much money as we need when I return!"

His mother couldn't help smiling at her son's youthful confidence.

"Don't worry, indeed! What else does a mother do when her son is about to leave her side for the first time?"

Moshe had no answer for that. Instead, he lifted his little brother, Yosef, from the wagon and swung him wildly through the air.

"Moshe!" squealed Yosef.

Then, more gently, Moshe picked up three-year-old Miriam. She threw her chubby arms around his neck and hugged him with all her might. Suddenly, a lump formed in Moshe's throat. He blinked hard, swallowed a few times, and handed Miriam over to Mama.

"Well," he said brightly, "who wants to see the big ship?"

Yosef took Moshe's hand. "But why do you have to go so very far? Papa traveled to closer places."

"You know why," Moshe answered. "Africa is the best place to buy certain goods to sell when I come back."

"Like cork?"

Moshe stopped short and stared at his little brother. "Where did you hear that?"

Yosef looked a bit sheepish. "I heard you talking to Meneer Jacobs about it."

"Yosef, I'm the man of the family now, and you'll listen to me. Not one word about anything you ever heard me say to Papa's partner about business. You could ruin everything for all of us!"

Yosef's eyes grew narrow; he glared up at his older brother. "I will not ruin anything!"

Esther Levi stepped in to smooth things over, as she always did when her two headstrong boys challenged each other. How alike they were, with her husband's dark eyes and intelligent minds.

"Moshe, that's enough. Yosef is ten, and he's old enough to understand about keeping important conversations private. Isn't that right, Yosef?"

The young boy nodded sullenly.

But Moshe was still frowning. "Mama, Meneer Jacobs is counting on me to strike a good deal on importing cork from Africa. Our whole fortune depends on secrecy."

Mama looked sharply at Moshe. "Our whole fortune depends on Hashem, or G-d, my son. Never forget that. And why Papa's partner would send a boy to Africa instead of going himself… well, let's say no more about it."

Moshe's annoyance vanished as quickly as it had come. He threw an arm around Yosef's thin shoulders. "Mama is absolutely right. Everything depends on Hashem. Still, you won't say a word, will you, Yosef?"

"Of course not! And when you're gone, I'll be the man of the family!"

Moshe turned to hide a smile. "You certainly will be. That's why I'm counting on you to listen to Mama and help her with Miriam."

"I guess I can help with Miriam. But you

really need me to keep an eye on things for you. Don't worry; I will."

Moshe rolled his eyes, but said nothing. He was struck speechless by the sight of the ship up close. Sailors climbed up and down the rigging, passengers jostled each other as they scrambled aboard, and porters carried crates and trunks up the ramp and onto the huge sailing vessel.

"There's my trunk; Meneer Jacobs packed all the business papers for me. He even sent a porter from the warehouse to load it aboard."

"Meneer Jacobs has been very kind to us," Mama said. "I'm sure you will represent him honestly and well on your travels."

"Well, I don't like him," Yosef grumbled. "He stares at me whenever I come into the warehouse with a message for Moshe."

Moshe secretly agreed with his little brother. Meneer Jacobs wasn't very friendly. He had a cold stare that could be intimidating.

"Well, he'll like all of us much more if

I complete a successful business deal on his behalf."

Suddenly the ship's bell sounded. Little Miriam covered her ears.

Moshe dropped his pack and turned to bid his mother farewell. "It's only a few months, Mama. I'll be back before you know it."

Esther smiled her approval at her son's words. "You will." Her voice broke, just for a moment, and her eyes grew bright. "But just in case things take longer than you expect, do take this package with you."

Curious, Moshe reached out to take the flat bundle.

"Inside are matzot, a Haggada, and a small flask of wine," Mama said calmly, "just in case."

"Oh, Mama! I should be back long before Pesach – before Passover!"

"Take it with you," she said firmly. "I'll rest easier knowing that you are prepared."

Esther could not help but feel uneasy about

this trip. After all, so many dangers could come up on a sea journey! Pirates, bad weather… she shuddered to think about it.

The ship's bell sounded again, and the last remaining passengers hurried aboard.

"Come, children." Mama tried to smile. "Let us say goodbye to your brother and wish him success. We hope his trip is short and that he returns safely."

Moshe slapped Yosef on the back and kissed little Miriam's curls. He turned to Mama last of all, hugging her as if he never wanted to let go.

"All aboard!" The booming voice of the captain's first mate rang out loud and clear. Not trusting himself to say any more goodbyes, Moshe picked up his heavy pack and headed straight up the gangway onto the ship.

Once on deck, Moshe turned to get a last glimpse of his dear family. He was determined to make his fortune so that he could support and take care of them. He was sure his father would have been proud.

How Moshe missed Papa at moments like this! How he needed his wise advice!

Well, as Mama had reminded him, it all depended on Hashem, his Father in Heaven.

"Please, Hashem," he whispered, "keep my family well while I travel. Make my voyage successful, and bring me back safely to them!"

Chapter Two
On Board

The passengers slowly made their way below deck to settle in for the journey ahead. Moshe looked around, but didn't see a single familiar face.

"No one from town mentioned an upcoming trip. I might be the only Jew aboard," he thought.

The crew pointed the way to his quarters, and Moshe dragged his bags into a small, bare room. It was dark and musty, and smelled of damp wood.

At least I have my own space. Moshe stowed his belongings under a narrow wooden bunk that was attached to the wall. He covered the thin straw mattress with a linen sheet from home, and folded a blanket neatly on top.

Some smooth boards nailed to the opposite wall served as a table, and Moshe placed a small locked trunk on top. Inside were his precious tefillin, which he always put on for his daily prayers, as well as the bread, dried fruit, and smoked fish and meat he'd brought along for the journey. Moshe shook his head and smiled as he stowed his Pesach bundle safely on a shelf. Surely he'd be home long before Pesach!

The ship lurched, and Moshe felt his stomach lurch along with it. Stopping to steady himself, he went back through the narrow passageway and up on deck. The salty air was refreshing, and the frantic activity on deck was interesting to watch.

"Hoist the sail! Fasten the yardarm!"

Moshe stood well out of the way of the crew as the sailors scurried about, performing their various tasks. He said Tefillat Haderech – the Traveler's Prayer – as the ship set out on its journey. It was an exhilarating feeling to be on his own for the first time… exciting and just a bit scary.

* * *

After a full day of sailing, there was nothing to see but ocean on all sides and the unchanging line of the horizon. As the sun grew lower, the sky glowed with orange and purple streaks of light. After a dinner of one of Mama's meat pies, Moshe went below and whispered the nighttime prayer of Shema. Too tired to feel the hard wooden planks beneath him, Moshe settled into his bunk and pulled the blanket over his shoulders. He closed his eyes, and let the motion of the ship rock him to sleep.

The voices of the crew members woke Moshe the following morning. He groaned and rolled over, hugging his middle. With great difficulty, he tried to stand upright and dress, but the movement of the waves set his head spinning.

For the first time since setting sail, Moshe wished he were back home.

He said the morning prayers with great feeling, and then slowly and painfully made his way up to the deck. He couldn't eat anything, but gulped great breaths of the fresh sea air.

Moshe gratefully took a dipper of clean water from the galley assistant.

The young sailor shook his dark head sympathetically. "It's rough on the sea, it is. But you'll get used to it. My first trip, I couldn't eat for days. You need anything, just ask me. Name's Henrique."

"Thank you, Henrique," Moshe croaked. He slipped a small silver coin into the kind sailor's hand. It couldn't hurt to have a friend on board.

Moshe closed his eyes and leaned against the side of the ship. He could feel the water sloshing inside him. How he longed for dry land beneath his feet!

Moshe spent the rest of the morning sitting on the deck. From time to time, he wiped his face with water. In the afternoon, Moshe walked around the deck several times, clutching the ship's sides for support, trying to catch a sea breeze against his flushed face.

"Greetings, where are you from?"

Moshe turned to see a broadly built young man with bright red hair. He extended his hand, and Moshe gripped it feebly.

"I hail from Amsterdam," Moshe smiled weakly at the stranger, "and you?"

"I am from Haarlem, and my name is Jan," replied the young man. "I deal in silk cloth and hope to sell my wares in different ports on this voyage. What's your trade?"

"My partner and I import and export various goods," Moshe replied. He didn't want to say too much about cork. What would stop someone else from trying to buy cork and take away his business?

"I see," Jan answered. "Well, I hope you'll be successful. It's a long journey, and everyone here hopes it will be worth the trouble."

Moshe continued on his walk around

the ship and discovered that several men were traveling to North Africa. Others planned to continue on to more distant locations.

Moshe's routine was the same for the first few days. Below deck he still felt dizzy and ill. He remained on deck in the fresh sea air as much as he could, watching the vast ocean.

As he grew accustomed to the rocking and swaying of the ship, Moshe was able to spend some time each day in his quarters, reviewing his business papers and plans. He always took great care to lock them in his trunk, away from prying eyes.

Moshe pictured the joy on Mama's face when he would return with valuable contracts for cork, earning enough money to last for years! How happy the children would be when he would shower them with gifts! Resting on the hard boards of his bunk, Moshe smiled to himself, thinking of his beloved family.

* * *

The days passed slowly. Moshe and the other passengers grew weary of the long trip, anxious to reach their destination.

"Tell me please," Moshe called out to Henrique, "I see land! Is that the coast of Africa?"

The young sailor shook his head. "Oh, no. Not yet. A day or two to the Atlantic Ocean. Then through to the Strait of Gibraltar. After that, to the Alboran Sea and on to the northern coast of Africa."

Moshe nodded. "If we have not passed through the Strait yet, what land do I see?"

Henrique squinted in the bright sunlight. "That's the coast of Spain."

"Spain!" Moshe thought. He shivered. Moshe recalled the many stories he'd heard of Jewish families that fled Spain to escape the Inquisition and live openly as Jews. "I can't imagine what it is like for Jews still in Spain, may Hashem watch over them."

He stared at the coastline until he could

see it no longer, thinking of his fellow Jews who lived in such a cruel place.

It was just as the sun was starting to set when Jan joined Moshe on deck.

"Smooth as glass," Jan noted. "On my last voyage, the ship tossed to and fro for days like a leaky pot in the ocean. We were lucky to reach our destination that time!"

"We are fortunate that this journey has been so calm," Moshe remarked. "I need smooth sailing all the way to Africa and all the way home again!"

"No worries," Jan replied. He gestured toward the still waters stretching as far as the eye could see. "Smooth as glass," he repeated.

Full of high hopes, Moshe bid his fellow traveler good night. He would not have been so confident had he looked up at the sky before going below deck. But he had not seen the dark storm clouds swirling in the distance, so he fell into a peaceful sleep.

Chapter Three

Disaster at Sea

"Crack!" An earsplitting clap of thunder woke Moshe in his berth a few hours later. The ocean tossed the wooden ship as if it were a child's toy! Moshe tried desperately to leave his cramped cabin and see what was happening. But the wild lurching of the ship threw him back onto his narrow bunk.

Henrique appeared at the door, his hair wet, his eyes wide with fear.

"Stay below deck, Captain's orders! All passengers below deck!"

"Henrique," Moshe cried, "what's happening?"

"Bad storm... worst I've ever seen." In a flash, the sailor was gone, back to his post.

Moshe clung to his bunk. The waves hurled the ship from side to side. The wind howled and screamed.

Sailors yelled over the wind and scurried

about to batten down the hatches and secure the lines. Moshe wondered how they could ever hold onto the wet, slippery ropes. *How could they keep the sails from tearing? Would the ship lose the battle against the powerful storm?*

His cabin was dark. With each huge wave, water roared down into the ship. Moshe hung onto his bunk with all his might. Above the shrieking of the wind he sobbed and prayed.

How foolish were all his hopes and dreams of riches! Now, all he wanted was one thing only: to be saved from this storm, to live!

"Please, Hashem, save me! Bring me home to Mama and my family!"

Hours seemed to pass. The ship creaked and groaned with each massive wave. Suddenly, in the darkness of his cabin, Moshe felt his bunk loosen and fly off the wall! Without anything solid to hold onto, Moshe was thrown back and forth like one of Miriam's rag dolls.

With no one to reassure him, Moshe spoke

out loud. "I can't stay here any longer. I have to see what is happening on deck."

Slipping and sliding, Moshe bravely made his way out of his cabin.

"Where is everyone?" he wondered. Clinging to the stairs, he slowly made his way up to the top deck. The rain was relentless. He closed his eyes to avoid the angry gusts of wind. Giant waves rocked the ship wildly from side to side. Moshe swayed and fell on the slippery boards.

"Henrique! Jan!" Moshe looked around for any sign of life. Where was the crew? Were they below deck with the passengers? Had they all been washed overboard into the sea?

Moshe steadied himself and took a deep breath. Once again, he looked around but he did not see anyone. The wind was so strong that the cold rain seemed to be hitting him from every direction. Moshe could barely see anything at all.

"Help! Is anyone there? Help me!" There

was no response, and his hoarse cry faded in the blustery wind. A bright flash of lightning lit up the ship. Suddenly, Moshe could see there was no one else on the rainy deck. He was all alone.

Fear hit him like a punch to the stomach. For a moment, he couldn't move or breathe. *What can I do?* Just then, a high wave came crashing over the side of the ship and knocked Moshe off-balance.

Thrown to his knees, he began crawling across the slippery planks. *Was there a place to hide, something to hold onto? Wood! Wood floats!* With trembling hands, Moshe felt his way along the railing to the nearest wooden beam.

With the wind whipping at him and the cold rain beating against his face, Moshe struggled to untie his corded belt. It took a few tries to wrap the belt around his shaking body and tie himself to the sturdy beam.

"There! The belt is as tight as I will be able to make it!" Moshe's body sagged from the effort. He locked his arms around the beam.

Moshe rode out the storm, hanging onto that beam for dear life. The fragile ship was engulfed in water as huge waves rolled on board. Moshe felt himself thrown from side to side at the mercy of the ocean's fury. Over and over, the ship rolled dangerously, as though it were about to sink. Then, at the last minute, the waves whirled in the other direction; the ship stood upright. Then the next huge wave would come along.

The beams of the ship creaked and groaned. It sounded as if the ship would break apart in the violent storm. Would this torture never end? Moshe kept forcing himself to scan the deck for other passengers or sailors, but there was no one to be seen. He was bruised and sore, wet and freezing.

With a mighty heave, the ship began to groan and shudder. The once proud vessel began to crack at its joints! One moment, Moshe was on the rainy deck; the next moment, he was thrown overboard, still attached to the beam. The shock of hitting the water made him gasp for breath. But the wood floated, and Moshe clung to it desperately. *If I want to see my family, I have to stay strong!*

Over and over, the waves crashed above him. Gagging on the salty ocean water, he kept pulling himself to the surface to take a breath. His arms grew numb from the cold, and the waves gave him no rest. As he braced himself for the next wave, Moshe thought about his family, giving him the strength to continue. *I will not let the storm beat me; I will not!*

The storm pushed through its fury and then, just as suddenly as it had begun, the wind grew softer, and the powerful rain slowed to a light drizzle. By this time, Moshe was exhausted. He leaned his head against the beam, afraid to close his eyes, desperate to stay awake and to survive.

"Thank You, Hashem," he whispered. "Please bring me safely ashore."

Chapter Four
Alone in a Strange Land

Even before he opened his eyes, the blazing heat of the sun woke Moshe. Flies buzzed loudly next to his ear and around his face.

Then it hit him. *Where am I?* He felt damp sand beneath his body. He struggled to sit up, but something prevented him from moving.

Moshe looked down. The beam was still tied to him with his twisted belt. It took several minutes to untie it, as his hands and fingers were swollen and red from the sun. He must have bobbed around in the ocean for hours, then washed ashore.

As he sat up, slowly and painfully, Moshe whispered, "Thank You, Hashem. It is only through Your miraculous kindness that I am alive!" He bowed his head and thought of all the other passengers, and the brave captain and sailors who were lost in the violent storm.

Moshe stood up carefully. His wiggled

his arms and legs, and nothing seemed to be broken. He felt bruised all over. His hair was stiff, encrusted with sand and dried seawater. His clothing was tattered; his shoes were gone. But the most overwhelming feeling was thirst. Moshe's throat was on fire. He swayed on his feet. He was weaker, thirstier, and hungrier than he'd ever felt in his life. This was bad. How would he find shelter, or fresh water, or food?

"I'm sure Hashem saved me for a reason," he thought. "I can't give up now!"

With renewed focus, Moshe looked around. He was on a beautiful stretch of sandy beach that seemed to go on as far as the eye could see. "The water looks calm and blue today," Moshe thought, "but it's not fit to drink!"

Moshe turned away from the shore and continued to scan the area. In the distance were clusters of tall trees. "Where there are trees, there may be edible plants and fresh water," he thought. "I'll head in that direction."

Moshe walked slowly, his bare feet sore

and swollen. Every few minutes, he paused to gather strength. It took hours to reach the first cluster of trees. There was a small brook running along the path, and Moshe said a heartfelt bracha – a blessing – before drinking. The water was warm, but it wasn't salty. Moshe wanted to drink endlessly, but he knew better. "If I drink too much, I'll get sick," he thought. "I'll just swallow a few mouthfuls, and wait for a bit."

In the meantime, Moshe washed his face and soaked his aching feet in the stream. After drinking a bit more, Moshe said whatever prayers he could recite by heart while resting in the shade.

He found a branch he could use as a walking stick, and decided to follow the path of the brook. "Perhaps it will lead me to a farm or a village!"

Leaning on his stick, Moshe kept walking. The sun was almost straight overhead when he saw some red-roofed buildings in the distance.

His heels were cracked and bleeding.

He felt sharp pain with every step, but Moshe wouldn't give up. "I've been saved for a reason," he kept thinking. "I need to get back home to my family."

Finally, Moshe approached the outskirts of a town. The center square boasted a busy marketplace filled with rows and rows of wooden stalls, some with covered roofs of bright, colorful material. There was a large well nearby, where several women were filling up wooden buckets with water to bring home. Their young children played near the well, laughing and splashing in the puddles.

Moshe did not realize how battered and bruised he looked, until the townspeople began to point and gesture. By the time he reached the group, more and more people had gathered. He tried to speak to them, but not a single person understood Dutch, the language of Moshe's beloved Amsterdam.

Desperately thirsty, Moshe held up his hand, shaped like a cup, and pretended to drink.

"Agua," said one motherly looking woman in the crowd. She stepped forward and offered Moshe some water.

Moshe smiled and bowed his thanks. He whispered a bracha, then finished off the water. Next, he formed the shape of a boat with his hands. He lifted his hands up and down, to mimic the storm on the ocean. Then he pulled his hands apart, to show that the boat had sunk.

The people's eyes grew wide. One woman said something to her young son and pointed to a nearby building. Her son pulled Moshe by the hand, leading him to the building. It was coated with yellow clay, and had a courtyard in the front.

A tall, dark man wearing a leather apron greeted Moshe in French. Moshe smiled, but shook his head. He didn't know enough French for a real conversation. Next the man tried another foreign word. Moshe shook his head again. Then, suddenly, came a familiar Dutch greeting!

Moshe smiled broadly, relieved that there was someone here who could understand him.

The man smiled back, and, in a very slow and halting Dutch, said, "They tell me that you are a survivor of the shipwreck. I congratulate you on your fortunate escape! Allow me to introduce myself. I am Juan, the owner of the largest inn of our humble town. I often entertain guests from other countries. That is why I know several languages. It would be my pleasure to escort you to my inn. I will find you some clothing, and you must rest."

Moshe gratefully accepted the kind offer and allowed Juan to lead the way. "*Dank je*, thank you very much for your kindness."

Moshe felt as if he had entered a strange dream. He had no clothes, no money, and no way to get home.

"Please tell me where I am. I was heading to Africa when the storm hit. Am I anywhere near Africa?"

Juan looked down at the boy with compassion. "You are in Spain," he answered, "the best and most powerful country in the world."

Moshe's head felt light and dizzy. He swayed and held onto his walking stick.

Quickly, Juan led Moshe to a bench at the inn. He held a cup of strong tea to the boy's pale lips. Then, he half carried him to a small room and laid him down on a straw mattress.

"Spain?" Moshe thought. "It's the last place on earth I should ever want to be!"

Sick with despair, weak and exhausted, Moshe closed his eyes and slept.

* * *

When Moshe awoke, the sun was low in the sky. At first he couldn't remember where he was or how he got there. Then the events of the past few days came back in a rush. Shipwrecked in Spain, of all places... what was he to do?

"One thing at a time," Moshe decided.

He noticed that a cloth and a pitcher of water had been left for him. Moshe washed his hands, discarded his tattered clothing, and scrubbed himself clean from head to toe. He found a worn shirt and other garments piled on a chair and gratefully put them on. Only then did Moshe take the time to look around him.

The room was not much larger than the berth Moshe had on the ship, but it was furnished with a wooden chair and a bed. There was one window overlooking the marketplace, and most of the stalls were closed for the day.

"How long will Juan allow me to stay here without paying?" he wondered. "I will have to work to earn my keep and save money for the trip home. And I must start right away."

Moshe smoothed his white shirt, straightened his cap, and carefully made his way down to the dining area. Juan was serving his guests, and many of the tables were filled with travelers and other townspeople. The room grew quiet when he entered.

"There you are!" Juan said. "Just in time for roast rabbit and a drink of ale!"

Moshe turned pale as he heard the offer

from the innkeeper. "No thank you," he said with a strained smile, "I would prefer a simple diet of bread and fresh vegetables; I am not used to such rich foods."

"As you wish." Juan set some bread and vegetables in front of Moshe, but looked at him strangely. What hungry young boy wouldn't eat meat to regain his strength?

Moshe thanked him, washed his hands for his meal, and secretly whispered the bracha on his food. His mind was working feverishly. When Juan sat down next to him for a moment, Moshe had a plan.

"Señor Juan, my kind friend, I cannot sleep here and eat your food for free. Please give me work to do. I can sweep, and serve, and tend to your chickens. Anything is good enough for me. I need to earn the fare for my trip back to Amsterdam."

Juan nodded, pleased with the offer. "I see you are a gentleman. I will allow you to work here and make your home under my roof for as long as you need."

Moshe breathed a sigh of relief. He had clothing on his back. He had shelter and food. Somehow, he trusted this simple innkeeper.

"So, señor, how often do ships lay anchor here? When can I expect to find passage home?"

"Our small town has mostly small fishing boats," Juan explained. "Only once in a long while do large ships enter our harbor."

Moshe's face fell. "I want to go home as soon as possible. My family will be sick with worry when my ship fails to arrive."

Juan looked puzzled. "You have a place to sleep, eat, and work. The time will pass quickly. You will love it here in our little village. You'll see."

Moshe forced himself to smile. "Yes! Thank you! I am indeed fortunate, señor."

Moshe's mind was working frantically. Mama had been right. He might not be home for Pesach. With his bundle of matza and wine lost at sea, what was he going to do?

Trying to look calm and casual, Moshe chose his words carefully. "So, please tell me more about your beautiful village. Are there any Jews in the area?"

In an instant, Juan's open, friendly face turned dark and stern. "Jews?" he said distastefully. "Thank the Lord, there have not been Jews in Spain for generations! We are all of the one true religion here. We have cleansed Spain of every last Jewish heretic. You may find some other foreigners in our town, but one thing I promise you, you will not find a single Jew here, and I say good riddance!"

Moshe's stomach clenched. This was enemy territory. It was not safe to do anything that could give away his identity as a Jew. He could trust no one.

Chapter Five
A Plan of Action

As the weeks and months passed, Moshe never let himself grow too comfortable. He found clever ways to keep Shabbat and eat kosher food without arousing suspicion. One spring evening, Moshe made his way out of the inn and sat down on a bench in the courtyard to polish the guests' boots. Here he was, a young boy alone in a strange country, a country in which Jews were not welcome, and Mama's fears had come true. The arrival of spring meant it was almost Pesach.

In any other land, he would find a nice Jewish family who would invite him for the Seder and provide him with matza and wine, maror and charoset. But in Spain, that could never happen. Moshe sighed. *If only I could find a Jewish family…*

Suddenly, Moshe remembered something. He heard that not all Jews had left Spain. Some were still here, acting just like the non-Jews on the outside, but living as Jews in secret. If anyone suspected they were really Jews, their lives would be in great danger.

"What if I could find a hidden Jewish home?" Moshe wondered. "Then I could have a real Pesach. How can I go about uncovering such a well-kept secret?"

The lights at the inn winked out one by one, and still Moshe remained outside, lost in thought. *If I were a Jew in Spain before Pesach, where would I be?*

A thought came to him. Moshe smiled into the darkness. Tomorrow, he would begin his search for a secret Seder. And now, he knew just where to start looking!

* * *

The next morning, Moshe rose early, said his prayers, and rushed through his chores. Casually, he asked, "Señor Juan, do you need anything from the marketplace? I will gladly go and fetch whatever you like."

Juan smiled at the boy's eagerness. "You want even more jobs?"

"Yes, señor," Moshe answered. "The more I work, the faster I can earn money to return home."

"Very well," replied the innkeeper. "Buy ten sacks of wheat in the market, load them on my donkey, and take them to the mill. Have the wheat finely ground for baking."

"Right away, señor," said Moshe.

Juan pulled out a few silver coins and looked deeply into Moshe's eyes. "Until now, I have paid the miller myself, but you have been here some time already. I trust that you will deal fairly and honestly with me."

Moshe drew himself up to his full height. "I owe you so much," he replied. "You gave me food and clothing and a roof over my head. I will treat your money as carefully as if it were my own."

Juan nodded, pleased with this answer. "Take along something to eat in the marketplace. I will expect you back at sundown."

"Thank you. *Gracias*, Señor Juan." Moshe placed the coins in a pouch on his belt. He led the donkey out of the barn and made his way toward the center of town.

"How the mighty have fallen!" thought Moshe. "I started my trip to Africa with important papers, a business deal to conduct, and people to see. For months, I've been just an errand boy in Spain."

After loading the donkey with the sacks of wheat, he sat down under a shady tree to eat and rest. It was a busy market day with many townspeople coming to the market to buy, sell, and trade their many wares.

"Fresh bread! Hurry while it is still hot!" shouted the baker, his white apron gleaming in the sun.

"Fresh fruit and vegetables," yelled a farmer, showing off his fresh produce.

"Scarves and shawls in many colors," cried the voice of the weaver.

Moshe breathed in the perfume of fresh warm bread, the pungent scent of cinnamon, and the briny smell of fresh fish. It was time to put his plan in motion.

He ate slowly while carefully observing the people around him. Who would be the answer to his prayers? Whose actions would tell him what he needed to know?

An elderly woman in black walked toward the vegetable stall. She was leaning on a gnarled wooden cane as she walked slowly through the marketplace. At first, Moshe thought she might be the person he was waiting for. He cautiously watched her make some purchases. After arguing over the price with the short, ill-tempered fisherman, the woman bought a small fresh fish. Then she bought some greens and onions. Moshe pretended to look off into the distance, but he grew excited. Maybe this customer was shopping for a secret Seder!

The old woman then made her way to the bakery stall and purchased two large loaves of bread. Moshe slumped back in disappointment. He knew she couldn't be Jewish if she was buying bread so close to Pesach!

A moment later, Moshe noticed a young mother walking toward the marketplace with two small children. She purchased some fresh brown eggs from a farmer, and after carefully tucking them into her straw basket, she gently covered them with grass to keep the fragile eggs from breaking.

"Come, children," she crooned, "that is all we need today, let us head back home; your father will want a good meal!"

The baby was beginning to cry as the woman completed her small purchase and paid the vendor. The woman turned quickly, and as she tried to balance the unwieldy basket and her fussy baby, she lost her footing and nearly fell.

Moshe realized what was about to happen, and without thinking, he jumped up to help her and caught the basket of eggs before it hit the ground. The relieved woman smiled and thanked Moshe for his help.

"Señor," she said in a grateful voice, "if not for you, my child would have fallen and my eggs would have been lost. Thank you."

Moshe nodded, then rose to lead the donkey to the mill. He couldn't spend more time in the marketplace today. "So far, all I have done is rescue some eggs, but my own search is still far from over," he thought. "I knew it wouldn't be that easy. I will try again tomorrow."

The next morning, Moshe went on another errand for the innkeeper. At noon, he sat down and took out some vegetables for lunch. He ate slowly, trying to make his little meal last as long as possible. The sun was very bright, and Moshe squinted as he watched the shoppers in the market. He tried to hide his feeling of desperation, hoping for his plan to succeed; he truly had no other idea to try.

Moshe observed all the men and women

who came to the market and noticed exactly what they bought from each vendor. Farmers rode up with their wagons piled with fresh vegetables, fruit, and live animals to sell. He watched young children playing games as they waited for their mothers to finish their shopping.

Seeing the children caused Moshe to sigh. Were the children well back at home? How was Mama managing without him? When would he see them all again?

From a distance, Moshe noticed two women approaching the marketplace. They looked around uneasily, and he wondered why. One woman was taller than the other and wore a dark green robe with a colorful shawl around her shoulders. The shorter woman was dressed all in black. They stopped at the vegetable stand and in a loud voice, the taller woman asked for salad greens.

"Do you have fresh greens today?" she

asked in a rude voice. "The ones my maid purchased yesterday were wormy!" The farmer turned red with embarrassment.

"Pardon, Señora Maria," he stammered, "my vegetables are always fresh!"

"Fresh greens!" Moshe thought. "Is this the woman I've been waiting for?" Moshe was about to approach the woman when he saw something that made him sit back down. While Maria argued with the vegetable vendor, the other woman was secretly hiding other vegetables in her large flowing sleeves.

The farmer yelled, "Hey, there! Put those back!"

Moshe shook his head. "This woman is definitely not someone I wish to meet," Moshe said to himself with disgust. "She is nothing more than a common thief."

Moshe was beginning to think that his plan may have been too hopeful. He had to get back to the inn, where Juan would be expecting him to do the afternoon chores. Maybe he would have to start figuring out how to celebrate Pesach all by himself.

Suddenly, along came a fine carriage, driven by a coachman in a crisp gray uniform and pulled by a team of glossy white horses. It appeared in a cloud of dust on the main road and came to a stop at the marketplace.

Moshe sat up straight and paid close attention. The coachman nimbly jumped down from his seat and, with a flourish, opened the door. The townspeople quickly moved aside as the occupant of the carriage stepped out. Bowing with respect, the men and women in the marketplace murmured greetings to the tall man as he strode along.

It was obvious that this customer was someone important in the village. He had a square face with dark, intelligent eyes. His cloak was made of fine gray silk and he wore expensive, shiny leather boots.

The dignified man approached the marketplace and paused for a moment before approaching one of the stalls. The farmer greeted his illustrious customer with a flow of words and compliments.

"Good afternoon, señor, how are your dear children and your excellent wife? I am sure they are well. I hope your vineyards are all full and green." The man smiled kindly at the farmer and finally selected a generous assortment of fresh produce. Moshe watched all this with great interest.

After a few moments, the tall man returned to the carriage, and the coachman placed all the bundles inside.

With a loud crack of the whip, the carriage swept out of the marketplace and disappeared up the road. Moshe smiled and took a deep breath.

"If I had not seen that with my own eyes, I would have thought I dreamt it. Greens, bitter root vegetables... exactly what I have been looking for," he said to himself. "But now, there is no time to waste!"

Chapter Six
Moshe Takes a Chance

Moshe jumped up and hurried over to the closest stall at the market. He tried to act calm and natural, but inside, he was trembling.

"Señor, please tell me. Who was the man who just left in that beautiful carriage?"

"That was Carlos Romanus," the farmer replied. "He's the richest, most powerful man in our town – no, in the whole area – and a personal friend of the king. Not only does everyone know Carlos Romanus, but half the town works in his vineyards!"

"So, does he live around here?" Moshe asked.

The farmer smiled. "Of course, of course. Why, everyone in town knows where Señor Romanus lives, even the little children."

With a wide sweep of his right hand, the farmer asked, "Do you see that castle up on the hill? That is the Romanus Estate."

Moshe looked up to see a beautiful structure in the distance. He had noticed it whenever he did errands in the market. Although Moshe was from a big city and had seen many beautiful buildings, he had never seen a castle as large or as grand as the one that belonged to Carlos Romanus.

Watching him, the farmer nodded proudly. "And where does Señor Carlos Romanus buy whatever vegetables he does not grow in his own kitchen garden? From me!"

Moshe nodded thoughtfully. He needed time to plan and couldn't afford to make a mistake. Now that he had seen Señor Romanus and knew where he lived, the next part of his strategy was much more challenging.

"Thank You, Hashem, for Your kindness," Moshe thought. "Now, please help me in what I am about to do!"

* * *

That evening, as the sun was about to set, Moshe quietly slipped out of his room at the inn.

He paused at the doorway of his lodgings and looked around in all directions, satisfied that there was no one who would see him leave.

Moshe hurried along, hoping there was still time. He walked down the road through the marketplace and made his way up the mountain toward the house of Carlos Romanus.

The air was cool and dry, and a brisk wind swirled around Moshe as he climbed higher and higher. But Moshe was not bothered by the wind. He was on a mission, and he did not intend to let anything – or anyone – stop him. Moshe felt uneasy in the bright moonlight. His every step toward the house sounded too loud.   There was nowhere to hide.

Moshe reached the top of the private pathway and looked around. The castle was more impressive up close than it had been from the bottom of the mountainside. It was large, stately, and somewhat foreboding. As he walked to the door, Moshe noticed that there were no lights visible from the windows.

"I can't stop now, I have come too far," he encouraged himself. "I have to be right!" Moshe took a deep breath and knocked three sharp raps that broke the stillness. After a minute, a butler in full uniform opened the heavy front door.

"Please, I would like to speak to the master of the house?" Moshe asked in a trembling voice.

The servant gazed coolly at the unexpected visitor. He shook his dark head. "Señor Romanus is not available. Good night."

"Please, señor, I am a stranger in these parts, stranded after a shipwreck. I am desperate to see Señor Romanus, just for a moment!"

"I wish I could help you," the butler replied in an expressionless voice, "but my master is not receiving visitors this evening. He has retired for the night."

The servant closed the door firmly. Moshe knocked again.

The butler opened the door and stared disapprovingly at the stranger who would not leave.

"Señor Romanus sets appointments between the hours of ten o'clock and noon. You may return then. *Buenas noches.*"

"Please have pity on a lonely stranger. I do not know anyone here. All I ask is a few minutes of your master's time." Moshe's voice rose in desperation. He simply did not know what else to do.

At that very moment, Carlos Romanus appeared in the hallway. His face looked pale and strained. "Who is it, Manuel?"

Before the servant could answer, Moshe called out, "Please, señor, won't you see me for just a few moments on urgent business?"

Señor Romanus motioned for his servant to allow Moshe to enter. The boy was trembling and sweating. He tried to compose himself in the wide, richly decorated hallway.

Carlos Romanus turned to the butler. "You may go."

The perfectly trained servant obeyed instantly. He bowed his head and turned to leave.

But for just an instant, he gazed at his master with a strange look that made Moshe uneasy. Moshe's mouth was dry with fear as he watched the man glide silently down the hallway.

Carlos Romanus led Moshe into a magnificent room covered in luxurious wooden panels and filled with gleaming candelabras. He closed the door and turned abruptly to Moshe.

"You sounded quite determined to speak to me. What could possibly be so important that you insisted on coming so late?"

The wealthy landowner sounded calm, but his eyes narrowed suspiciously.

Moshe took a deep breath. "Please, Señor Romanus, my name is Moshe ben Chayim from Amsterdam and..." He paused for a moment and continued in a whisper, "...and I would like to join your Seder."

"My what?" exclaimed Carlos Romanus. "I have no idea what you are saying!"

"I am a Jew," Moshe continued simply,

"and I am stranded here with no family and no kosher food for Pesach. You are my only hope."

Carlos laughed and shook his head. "Young man, now I know that you are surely a lost soul. There are no Jews here. Everyone knows that Jews were expelled from this country and none remain. You have come to the wrong place. You have come to the wrong man."

"I don't believe you," Moshe whispered fiercely. "You are a Jew. I saw you in the market. You bought bitter herbs, *maror*, for a Seder!"

Carlos Romanus grabbed Moshe's arm and squeezed it in a hard grip. "How dare you? Who sent you here to endanger my family? Who's behind these ridiculous accusations?"

Moshe began to cry. "Please believe me. I'm all alone. No one sent me, and I don't want any trouble." His voice broke. "I just want a Seder."

Carlos loosened his grip and stepped back. He was breathing hard, staring at Moshe's tear-stained face. He betrayed no emotion at all. At last, he spoke.

"You are a clever boy. I should have been more careful in the market."

Moshe wiped his face on his sleeve and waited.

"Very well," said the older man. "Be quiet, and come with me."

The boy trembled as he followed Carlos Romanus. They walked silently, first down one long dark corridor and then another. Moshe's heart was pounding in his ears. *What if I made a mistake? If this powerful man is not really a Jew, he could be leading me into a terrible trap! If he is a Jew and thinks I'm his enemy, what will he do to me? Hashem, You have taken me this far, please do not desert me in my time of need!*

Finally, Carlos went into a well-appointed sitting room, closed the door, and bolted it behind them. There were comfortable couches arranged on a beautifully designed carpet. Carved wooden cabinets displayed precious silver items. This room was completely isolated from the rest of the house.

"Even if I screamed," thought Moshe, "no one would hear me."

His fear left him, and he suddenly felt calm. It was too late now. He just had to go forward.

Carlos Romanus opened one of the cabinets and pressed a panel on the inside. To Moshe's amazement, the entire cabinet moved aside to reveal a doorway! The two walked silently down a narrow flight of stairs. Small candles in simple holders lit the way, casting an eerie glow in the tight space. At the bottom of the staircase was a heavy black door.

"What a perfect place to lock up an enemy," Moshe thought.

He held his breath as the older man slowly opened the door.

* * *

Moshe gasped with relief. It wasn't a prison, but a beautiful room draped in dark fabric and bathed in candlelight. A richly dressed woman and two young children sat at a small dining table. The woman looked searchingly at Moshe's face, then turned questioningly to Carlos Romanus.

He smiled at her and said, "My dear wife, G-d has answered our prayers and sent us a Pesach guest. Bella, this brave and clever young man is Moshe ben Chayim from Amsterdam. Please welcome him to our Seder!"

Señora Bella Romanus said, "This is such a pleasant surprise for all of us." She gestured toward the two children and introduced them.

"Our son is Diego, and our little girl is Rita."

Moshe smiled at his new friends. "Thank you for having me," he said.

The host turned to his son. "Quickly, Diego! Fetch a goblet for our guest, and let us begin the Seder!"

Although the feeling in the room was festive, no one spoke above a whisper. Walking like someone in a dream, Moshe took a seat at the table. He still couldn't believe his incredible good fortune. *Am I really at a Seder table of secret Spanish Jews?*

Carlos briefly explained that his family had been living as hidden Jews for generations, although publicly they lived just as the Spanish people all around them.

"Do you mean that this hidden room is the only place where you are able to act as Jews?"

His host sighed. "Yes, Moshe, this is how we are forced to live, and without moments like these, our lives would be worthless. Even though it is dangerous, what kind of Jews would we be if we did not have a Seder?"

"It's my first one," Rita said, her eyes shining.

"That's right, daughter," Bella said in a serious tone. "You're big enough now to keep our secret."

Moshe had tears in his eyes as he thought of his own younger brother and sister back home, having their Seder without him. He felt that this little Spanish boy and girl needed him even more at this moment.

He smiled at the Romanus family. "I am humbled to be at your Seder. Thank you for trusting me."

It was overwhelming and inspiring for Moshe to see what kind of Seder they had put together. There was wine, and matza, bitter maror and vegetables to dip in salt water. These details had been passed down faithfully in the families of hidden Jews.

Still, Moshe realized that the order of the Seder and some of the Jewish Passover traditions were new to his host and hostess. They listened eagerly as their guest shared whatever he could with these sincere Jews who were, in spite of their wealth, still living in slavery.

"Thank you, Moshe," Carlos said softly. "My parents did what they could, but I know less than they did."

His wife continued, "And our children will know even less if we cannot leave this place. You were sent to us by G-d to…"

A sound overhead interrupted her words. Bella's face grew white, and she pulled her daughter close. Carlos put his finger to his lips. Diego looked stricken.

Moshe had almost forgotten the danger. His heart beat faster as panic rose in his chest. Had someone followed him here? Were they about to be discovered?

Moment by silent moment, they held their breath and waited.

At last, Carlos Romanus smiled. "No one's there. Let's continue."

All year long, Señora Romanus sat in luxury while maids served delicacies on expensive dishes. Tonight, however, she prepared and served the Seder meal with her own two hands. Rita helped her mother, and Diego sat proudly next to his father, trying to learn the traditional Seder songs. The children were enthralled to hear about Moshe's life in Amsterdam, a life lived openly in a community of Jews. As he concluded the Seder with the words *"L'Shana haba'ah b'Yerushalayim* – Next year in Jerusalem," Bella looked meaningfully at her husband, and Carlos sighed.

Moshe watched them with compassion. He had one more thing to say.

"Señor, I can never thank you enough for the best Seder of my life. But for as long as I'm in Spain, let me be useful to you. Let me teach you and your family whatever I can about Torah and mitzvot!"

The older man nodded, unable to speak.

Young Diego looked up in surprise. Could it be that his father – the great and powerful friend of the king, the rich and important Carlos Romanus – was crying?

Chapter Seven

Keeping Secrets

Late the following night, once all the guests at the inn were back in their rooms, Moshe retraced his steps up the hill to the home of Carlos Romanus. The hill did not seem quite as steep, because he knew that a beautiful Seder awaited him. This time, he had no trouble gaining entrance to the Romanus mansion. Carlos met Moshe at the front door and motioned for silence. "I've sent away the servants. There's no one here to disturb us," he whispered.

Together they walked down the hallway to the private room. From the corner of his eye, Moshe thought he saw someone at the end of the hall, but a closer look revealed only a shadow of the trees in the moonlight from outside. What a way to live! The constant fear, the endless suspicion… Moshe felt a tremendous respect for Carlos, his wife, and his children.

After closing the shutters and waiting for a few moments, the wealthy man opened the cabinet and pressed the secret panel. Just as it had last night, the narrow, hidden staircase came into view.

Tonight, Carlos insisted that Moshe take the seat of honor at the head of the table and lead the Seder. Step by step, Moshe explained the laws and customs of the Seder to the whole family. Diego and Rita were full of questions, and Moshe was honored to be the one to teach them about Pesach. Moshe was amazed that they could arrange a Seder at all and couldn't resist asking, "How is it that you have matza for the holiday?"

Señora Bella smiled. "We harvest the wheat and set some aside in this secret room. Before Pesach, we grind it ourselves and bake it in the dead of night. Even our most trusted servants don't know about it."

Moshe frowned. He knew his host was careful to keep his Judaism a secret, but with so

many servants, there were eyes everywhere. He looked around.

"Señor Carlos, do any of your servants know about this room?"

"Only the butler who let you in last night," answered Carlos Romanus, "and I trust him like a brother. Manuel has been with me since I was a boy, and his father served my father. You have nothing to fear. He is keeping watch for us right now."

Moshe said nothing, but he felt his stomach tighten. He had taken an instant dislike to the servant he'd met last night. Moshe smiled suddenly. That butler reminded him of someone back home… Meneer Jacobs, Papa's partner in Amsterdam. He had never really liked Meneer Jacobs, with that same cool manner and intense way of staring. But he was a good businessman, and Papa always worked well with him. *I hope he is taking care of everyone in my absence.*

"If you trust Manuel," said Moshe to his host, "I'm sure he is a true friend."

As they ate the Seder meal, Moshe taught the family holiday songs and told stories about Pesach. The Romanus family could feel the sweet joy of the Seder that night. Señora Bella sighed. "I am so grateful to you, Moshe, for finally filling in the details that my dear mother was unable to explain."

"It's been my honor," Moshe answered. He turned to his host. "Señor, what about you? Do you have any memories of Pesach from your childhood?"

"I do remember eating matza, but my elderly parents never felt safe enough to tell me anything about my true identity. Just before their passing, they told me we were Jews and pleaded with me not to forget G-d or His people. It was too risky to ask anyone else for information; whom could I trust? It was only with G-d's blessing that I met Bella, and she taught me whatever I know."

* * *

Moshe spent as much time as he could in the grand mansion up the hill throughout Pesach. In the privacy of the secret room, he addressed the children by their Hebrew names: David and Rivka. He shared his favorite stories from the Torah and Talmud with all of them; he sang Jewish songs and taught them to read the prayers in Hebrew.

"Never forget the people for whom you are named, David and Rivka," Moshe told the Romanus children. "Just as King David and Rivka from the Torah lived their lives with full faith in Hashem, all Jews are able to do the same. Keep your faith in Hashem, and surely you will one day be able to live freely as Jews."

"But how will that be?" David asked doubtfully. "We hear stories of hidden Jews just like us, important people like our father. They have been taken away from their homes and never heard from again. People in this village don't like Jews at all. I am afraid they will find out our secret!"

"Do not fear," Moshe replied with a voice more confident than he really felt. "Hashem will watch over you."

But as Moshe made his way down the winding path to the inn, he looked over his shoulder uneasily. Was he being followed? Did anyone suspect he was Jewish, and that he was teaching the children in secret?

Moshe stopped and listened. Was that a footstep behind him? He tensed and stood still in the darkness. A moment later, Manuel came up behind him.

"The master has asked me to escort you back to your lodgings," he said.

Moshe let out a deep sigh of relief.

"Thank you. It's a dark night, and I appreciate the company."

The two of them walked silently, until Manuel asked, "Are you soon leaving our village?"

"I hope so," Moshe answered. "It's no secret that I have to earn the money for my trip home, and that may take some time."

"I see," the butler said, looking intently at Moshe. "How much more do you need?"

Moshe thought feverishly. Why was Manuel asking all these questions? Had someone asked him to find out? Was it safe to answer?

"Why do you ask?" the boy blurted out.

"I was just... interested. I assumed you were going to ask my master for money, am I right?" The man's dark eyes stared into Moshe's face. "Isn't that why you come to visit so often? Isn't that why you are trying to make friends with the children?"

Moshe turned to the loyal butler. "I know you are only looking out for the well-being of your master and his family. I assure you that my only desire is for friendship, not for money. You know I was shipwrecked. You know I am all alone. How can you accuse me of acting dishonestly?"

Manuel just stared some more. Moshe looked back without blinking.

At last the servant spoke. "I see. It's just that making friends in this country comes with some... risk."

"I understand," Moshe said slowly. The two stopped at the door of the inn, and Manuel nodded and muttered a curt, "Good night."

Moshe went up to his little room and stayed awake for a long time. What did Manuel's warning mean? Did he want Moshe to stay away from the Romanus family for their protection? Or, was he warning Moshe against a hidden enemy?

Who posed the greatest threat: his new friend, Carlos Romanus, and his wife; the children, who might be too young to be careful; or Juan, the kind innkeeper? Would he regret making friends in this frightening land?

More than ever, Moshe couldn't wait to be back on a ship, sailing for home.

After much thought, Moshe decided to continue meeting with the Romanus children, teaching them whatever he could in the time he had left in Spain. "Who knows?" thought Moshe. "Maybe just for this reason, I was shipwrecked here. This must be part of Hashem's grand plan, and I will not be afraid."

Still, he took some precautions. From then on, Moshe came to the Romanus mansion only with a delivery of goods from the market. That way, he could slip in through the kitchen entrance. All through the spring and summer, the children understood that when a delivery arrived, so had their Torah teacher.

David and Rivka were bright and eager to learn. As often as they could, Carlos and his wife would join in the classes. Soon the entire family could read Hebrew, say basic prayers, and make brachot on food. Moshe moved on to explaining the mitzvot and meaning of each Jewish holiday, trying desperately to squeeze in as much information as he could. It was an unforgettable Rosh Hashana and Yom Kippur that year for all of them. Moshe had never said his prayers with such feeling or felt their meaning so deeply.

Carlos Romanus was very grateful. "You are giving us life," he always said. "I will never forget your bravery and your kindness."

* * *

As the month of September drew to a close, Moshe worked harder than ever to save the money for his journey home. When he entered the dining room at the inn one fall morning, Juan rushed over to him. "I have important news for you. The merchant ship that arrived in our harbor yesterday will load up and set sail next week. After that, the seas will be too rough for the voyage."

"Juan, thank you so much for your help all this time. You have taken very good care of me, and now you have given me the best news."

Moshe was overjoyed with the prospect of seeing his family again. He shook Juan's hand, and went to work even more eagerly than before. He purchased wagonloads of supplies for the inn and unloaded them all neatly and quickly. He cleaned the floor of the inn and polished the kitchen utensils until they shone.

With a mixture of sadness and excitement, Moshe made his way up to Carlos's home one last time. He sat with the family and tried his best to answer their questions about the Torah and Jewish living. He blessed them that one day soon they would be able to live open Jewish lives in safety.

"Moshe," Señora Bella whispered in a voice overcome with emotion, "we will never forget you and the precious gift of Torah that you shared with us. We thank Hashem for sending you to our doorstep and hope that you have a safe return trip to your family."

With tears in his eyes, Moshe stood up and said goodbye for the last time. Then, Carlos motioned for him to come down into the secret room. Curiously, Moshe followed him.

"What I'm about to show you is still a secret from my wife and children," said Carlos Romanus. "It's something I've been working on for a long time."

The older man drew aside the dark fabric that lined the cellar, revealing a wooden door to a cold storage room. Moshe stepped inside. Carlos held up a lantern that illuminated shelves of dried and preserved food, bags of grain, tools and other supplies. Moshe didn't see anything out of the ordinary.

Handing over the lantern, Carlos took hold of one of the shelves and pulled up with all his might. The entire wall swung outward, revealing a dark passageway. It was a secret within a secret!

Moshe squeezed into the space behind the shelf and was shocked to see a tunnel leading into the darkness. He looked quizzically at his companion, who took the lantern and motioned for Moshe to follow.

The tunnel was low and damp, supported by wooden beams to shore up the inside. It sloped downward, growing increasingly wet and cold as they walked.

At last, a blast of fresh air hit Moshe's face. They were nearing the end. A few more steps, and Moshe looked up in amazement. They were standing in a large cavern, and the sound of the sea could be heard echoing through it!

"What is this place?" Moshe whispered. "Who dug the tunnel? What is all this?"

Carlos smiled. "Manuel and I discovered this cave when we were young boys. It has an underground river leading to the sea. Together we dug the tunnel from the house to this quiet spot where we've built this..."

Carlos brought Moshe around a rocky corner of the cave. He proudly revealed a small ship complete with rigging and sails.

What do you think of it, Moshe? It's taken years to get all this ready. Rivka is finally old enough to make the journey. Quietly, I've begun to sell my possessions and some of my land. Soon I will be ready to set sail and begin my life anew! I had to show you... to ask you... would there be opportunities for me in Amsterdam? Meeting you has made my desire to leave that much stronger!"

Moshe shook his head in awe as he looked at the little ship. His eyes were shining. What a wonderful secret! The small vessel was large enough to hold the family and all their supplies for the journey. There really was a way they could start a new life!

"This is wonderful! Of course there are many people who would love to do business with you in Amsterdam. How the children would enjoy learning and playing with other Jewish boys and girls!"

"Come aboard!" Carlos said to Moshe. "I want to show you everything I've prepared."

The two of them grew excited as they approached the ship. Their voices grew louder as they discussed all the happiness that awaited once the Romanus family made its escape. They never noticed a shadow moving beneath the ship's deck. They never suspected they were not alone.

Chapter Eight

A Sad Farewell

It was Carlos Romanus who first realized that something was wrong. He stopped suddenly and frowned. Pulling Moshe close, he whispered, "Those tools... they weren't there last time I came. All those empty sacks don't belong here either."

Moshe felt the cold shiver of fear slide down his back.

Carlos put his fingers to his lips and ducked under the hull of the ship. Moshe nodded and followed. Someone was there! They could hear the hatch opening and see a flicker of light.

Carlos and Moshe strained to see in the darkness of the cave. Who could have discovered the ship in this well hidden spot?

Bravely, Carlos took a step forward and peered up at the figure on the deck. Then he startled Moshe by laughing and saying, "Manuel! How you frightened us!"

Moshe breathed a sigh of relief. It was only the trusted friend and partner of Carlos Romanus.

Manuel's voice echoed in the cave. "Master? What are you doing here?"

"I've come to show my good friend all that we've accomplished together! You can lead the way."

Manuel didn't move or answer, and Carlos Romanus grew impatient.

"Come on, my good man. What are you waiting for?"

Manuel said nothing. Three more figures emerged behind him. Carlos Romanus froze in place.

"Manuel," he said. "My dear friend, what are you doing? Who is with you?"

The servant handed the lantern to one of his companions. He approached the edge of the deck and grabbed the ship's rope.

"My dear friend," he sneered. "My plan

is complete. My companions and I will be rich from now on. Thanks to you, I can hire many more dear friends in the future who will wait on me and do my bidding!"

Carlos Romanus swayed and almost dropped the lantern. All these men had worked for him! Moshe recognized the two men who were in charge of the Romanus stable and the head groundskeeper. They loaded up the tools and sacks from the corner of the cave, then climbed aboard the sailing vessel.

"Don't expect you'll be reporting anything to the authorities, will you?" Manuel gloated. "How would you ever explain all this without giving yourself away, Jew?"

Moshe looked around for a weapon or a way to stop this evil band of men. There were still some shovels nearby, but he and Carlos were outnumbered and outwitted. They could only stand and watch helplessly as Manuel expertly steered the ship along the underground river.

The servants' laughter echoed in the cavern as they sailed away with the hopes and dreams of Carlos Romanus.

* * *

The terrible shock had knocked all the spirit out of the wealthy landowner. Stunned and defeated, he allowed Moshe to lead him up the damp tunnel and into the cold cellar.

The boy carefully pushed the wall of shelves back into place, closed the door, drew the curtains, and supported Carlos all the way back into the house.

Moshe poured a glass of water and made sure Carlos drank every drop. Carlos looked around, then moaned and held his head in his hands.

"Betrayed! How could I have been so blind?"

He ran over to the cabinets in the study. All the silver was gone!

Carlos Romanus moaned again. "I gave Manuel thousands of coins to purchase supplies

for my escape. I've sold land and made him my agent. He must have been stealing from me for years!"

Moshe hardly knew what to answer. "You wanted, no… you needed someone to trust. It's not your fault that he was the wrong man."

"I've known him all my life. I can't tell anyone about this. It's all over. It will take months to sort out what he's stolen. I may even be ruined. What can I do now?"

Moshe looked deeply into the eyes of his friend. "The Jewish way is never to give up hope. You still have much of your land and your family home. You can still arrange to sell what is left, and you can build another ship for your family's escape. I have no doubt that if you would have tried to leave, Manuel would have alerted the authorities, and your entire family would have been captured. You may have lost your lives."

As Moshe spoke, he could see some color return to Carlos's face.

"You are right," he said. "I am years older

than you, but you speak the truth. This will delay my plans, but not destroy them."

Carlos sat deep in thought. He seemed to gain control and return to his old self. Moshe glanced out the window. It was almost light, and his own ship sailed today!

Slowly, Carlos stood up and reached into a leather trunk next to his desk. "I know you are leaving for home," he said. "But before you go, please do me the honor of accepting this gift."

He unfolded a beautiful black coat of fine woven wool, a heavy, luxurious garment adorned with solid silver buttons.

"I couldn't possibly take this from you," said Moshe. "Not after you've lost so much."

Carlos smiled wanly. "My dear friend, I knew you would say that. But I can never repay you for all you have taught me and all that you've done for my children's Jewish future. When you wear the coat, it will remind you of my family and me. You can be sure that we will never forget you!"

With a sob welling in his throat, Carlos hugged Moshe and added, "I have one request that I ask you to honor. Even if the coat grows old and threadbare, never part from it. Always keep it as a reminder of your time in Spain."

Moshe held the coat close to him. "I give you my word, but give me yours in return: when you do leave this terrible place, assure me that you'll do everything you can to join me in Amsterdam!"

* * *

There was nothing more to say. Moshe and Carlos embraced for one final time, and holding the coat that Carlos had given him, Moshe slipped out the back door and down the path to the inn. With tears in his eyes, he said a silent prayer to keep his new friend and his dear family safe in this dangerous country.

Juan met Moshe at the door as Moshe descended with his small travel bag. "Young man, you have worked hard and earned your

trip home. However, if you should wish to return to Spain, there's always a place for you here."

Moshe shook the innkeeper's hand. "I'm honored by your offer. Thank you for your trust and your friendship."

Juan handed over a heavy bag. "I have packed some provisions for you to take on board for your journey. Don't worry; I have not put in any meat." Moshe smiled as he recalled that first day when he had to explain to Juan that he would not eat any meat at the inn.

With one last smile of gratitude and one last wave, Moshe left the inn and headed to the dock. Within a few hours, the ship left the port and headed out to the open seas.

Chapter Nine
The Trip Home

On the ship back to Amsterdam, Moshe kept to himself. Throughout the trip he was preoccupied with his Spanish adventure and could not stop thinking about Carlos Romanus and his family.

As he gazed at the horizon, Moshe's eyes grew misty. Would David and Rivka remember what he'd taught them? Would they all be able to escape Spain someday?

The days went by swiftly. On the final day of the voyage, Moshe was filled with excitement. As the ship slowly made its way into the harbor, he could see the familiar sights of his hometown. How he longed to see his family after all this time!

"This was one business trip I will never forget!" Moshe thought to himself.

A short time later, the ship dropped anchor and Moshe was able to disembark. News of

Moshe's miraculous survival had made its way through the town, and a small crowd gathered at the harbor to welcome him home. With a shout of happiness, Moshe spotted his mother and hurried toward her.

"A miracle! It's a miracle that you are alive," sobbed Mama. She pulled him into a tight embrace, tears streaming from her eyes. "Thank You, Hashem, for returning my son to me!"

Moshe dried his eyes and stepped back, turning to Yosef and Miriam, the brother and sister he'd left behind so long ago. He couldn't hide his surprise.

"Yosef, you're almost as tall as I am!"

"What about me?" Miriam spoke up. "Don't you think I'm tall?"

Moshe laughed and threw her into the air until she shrieked with joy.

"Come on, all of you," said their mother. "Time to go home."

Moshe couldn't believe that he was

actually back in his own city, riding in the wagon together with his beloved family. He couldn't stop looking at his younger brother and sister, amazed at how they'd grown. That's why it took Moshe some time to notice they were heading to a different part of town.

"Mama, this is not the way home! Where are you taking me?"

Yosef and Miriam grew silent. Mama cleared her throat and took Moshe's hand.

"My dear son," she began, "there have been a few... changes while you were away."

Yosef couldn't hold back. He leaned forward and clenched his fists. "I told you I never liked him!"

Moshe looked puzzled. "Liked who? What kind of changes?"

"It's not your fault at all. It wasn't anyone's fault," said Mama, looking sharply at Yosef. "No one knew what had happened to you, Moshe, and it was only natural..."

"It was mean," Yosef muttered under his breath.

Mama continued as if there hadn't been any interruption. "...only natural under the circumstances that Meneer Jacobs would find a new agent to send to Africa."

Miriam chimed in. "So we had to move. But I don't mind. I share a room with Mama now, and it's very cozy. I like it. Really, I do."

"I could have been the new agent!" Yosef cried. "He could have given me a chance to earn that money, and we could have kept our home."

Mama sighed, and Moshe quickly understood that this was a conversation they'd had many times. With no one actually working, his father's partner had been generous to support Mama and the children at all.

"Yosef, I'm sure you would have done a fine job taking my place, but how could Mama have spared you? After I failed to return, she needed you to be the man of the house and take care of the family."

Yosef gave his older brother a grateful smile, and Moshe smiled back. "Let's just be thankful that we are all together. We will surely make the best of our new situation."

Mama wiped away a tear, and Miriam reached over and hugged Moshe. As long as they were together, life would be good again. The wagon stopped in front of a narrow row house, and they made their way inside.

A fire burned in the fireplace, making the narrow room feel warm and welcoming. Moshe recognized some of the furniture and familiar objects, but he could tell that so much had been sold to keep food on the table.

"Well, Moshe," said Mama, "how do you like it? It's rather dark and cramped, I know…"

Moshe turned to her with tears in his eyes. "Mama, I met a family living in the grandest, most luxurious home you could imagine, and they would trade places with us in a heartbeat! At least here, in Amsterdam, we can live as Jews without risking our lives!"

They all sat down near the crackling fire, anxious to hear Moshe's story. He told them all his adventures, from the shipwreck to his miraculous rescue, from the secret Seder to the terrible day when Manuel betrayed the Romanus family.

Mama looked lovingly at Moshe. "Oh, my dear! How much danger you faced! What a life they have to lead…"

"If only I had been there," said Yosef. "I would have helped you jump on the boat and take it back!"

Miriam spoke up, too. "I wish I could be Rivka's friend."

* * *

Later, in the tiny room he would share with Yosef, Moshe unpacked his few belongings. He hung up his beautiful woolen coat and sighed. What was happening to his dear friends so far away in Spain? Would he ever see them again?

"That's a very fine coat," Yosef said. "Where did you get it?"

Moshe sighed again. "It was a gift from

my friend in Spain, and I treasure it. Tomorrow I will wear it when I ask Meneer Jacobs for work."

The next day, after the morning prayers, Moshe wrapped himself in his luxurious coat and took a deep breath. Would his father's partner give him the work he needed to support the family?

It was too expensive for Mama to keep a carriage, so Moshe walked to the business office on foot. He walked through the familiar doors and up the steps where he had played as a child.

"Meneer Jacobs! It's so nice to see you again!"

"And you, Moshe! It's a miracle that you survived when the ship went down. How can I help you?"

"Well, I still need to support my family, as my father trusted me to do. May I hope for the chance to return to work here?"

Meneer Jacobs stared at the floor. Moshe realized this was not a good sign. He waited, and finally, the older man answered.

"You have to understand, Moshe, that no one thought... I mean, we all assumed... not a single other person returned after the shipwreck. Our papers and contracts were all lost... new people were hired..."

Moshe felt his stomach drop. What would he do to earn money for food and firewood this winter? How would the family survive if he had no work?

Meneer Jacobs looked up. "I still need documents and packages delivered throughout the city. If you want that job, it is yours."

Moshe didn't hesitate. Although the work he did before his trip to Africa was much more important, he needed to take care of his family.

"Thank you. I accept."

Moshe tried to put his difficult experience behind him and enjoy being back home with Mama and the children. Yet, not a day went by that he did not think about Carlos and his family and say a prayer for their safety.

All winter, Moshe proudly wore his black woolen coat. It kept him warm each day as he worked. It kept him warm each night as he went to the synagogue to study Torah.

Most of all, wearing the coat made him feel closer to Carlos. If anyone commented on Moshe's coat, he would sometimes tell a small part of the story of his adventure, being careful not to mention the names of his friends far away in Spain.

As the cold of winter slowly melted into the bright beginning of spring, Moshe carefully hung his coat in the cedar closet. This year, Mama bustled about, happily preparing for Pesach with much more enthusiasm than the year before. It was as if she wanted to make up for the Pesach that Moshe did not spend with the family, the Pesach when they thought they'd never see him again.

"Moshe," Mama called to him one morning, "I can hardly believe it is a year since your frightening adventure at sea!" She shook her head. "At least this year there will be no business trips!"

Moshe sighed. "I've been thinking about Carlos more than ever as Pesach gets closer. I wish there was a way that I could help. My fear is that if I try to contact him, it may put them all in terrible danger."

"I understand, Moshe," Mama responded gently. "I keep them in my thoughts and my prayers all the time. It's difficult that we cannot reach out to them. We have to trust that Hashem will help, and that one day soon, they may be able to leave safely."

"Amen," Moshe replied, and his eyes filled with tears.

* * *

During the Seder, Moshe sat at the head of the table, hardly believing that the last Seder he conducted was two floors underground in Spain. While the family was enjoying the festive

Pesach meal, Moshe recounted his miraculous story to all the guests. They were spellbound at his experience and tried to imagine celebrating Pesach in mortal fear.

"How do hidden Jews keep Pesach without having a rabbi to teach them or a community to help them?" one guest wondered.

Moshe replied, "It is something that I would not have considered possible had I not seen it with my own eyes. There is much that has been forgotten, but they had matza, maror, and other Pesach foods. They kept what they could, everything passed down from father to son and mother to daughter." Everyone grew quiet, thinking about secret Jews trapped in Spain.

Moshe ended the Seder with a heart full of longing and a silent prayer that Carlos and his brave family would find freedom like the Jews of Egypt. He wished that they would successfully escape Spain and be able to live openly as Jews.

* * *

Just as Moshe was thinking of Carlos, Carlos and his family were thinking of Moshe. Rivka wondered if she would ever meet Moshe's sister and become her friend. David wondered if he would remember all that Moshe had taught him. Bella hoped Moshe had a safe journey back home. And Carlos was preparing for Pesach with more knowledge this year, thanks to Moshe.

"Carlos," whispered his wife late one night, "I wasn't able to store enough grain to grind into flour for matza. I am afraid that if I ask for more in town, they will become suspicious. I don't feel that I can trust anyone anymore."

"I know what you mean, Bella," Carlos answered. "Just this week, I was summoned to meet the king's minister who visited our town. He kept telling me about two families of secret Jews who were discovered and punished. He bragged about taking all their riches and property for the king's treasury. Why was he telling me this? Does he suspect us?"

"Oh, Carlos," cried Bella, forgetting for a moment that they were trying not to make noise. "What will become of us? What will become of our children?"

Carlos tried to calm his wife. "We have to trust in Hashem, but not take too many risks. We will secretly grind whatever grain we have and not look for more. I will not purchase greens in the market as I did last year. I planted a few in our own kitchen garden. We are fortunate that the only person who understood why I bought what I did was our dear friend Moshe. I sometimes think it was all a happy dream that he was here, until I hear our children talk about Moshe and the wonderful lessons he taught us."

Bella sighed. "I feel that every step we take is being watched, and I do not know how much longer I will be able to live this way! But for now, I will grind the grain and prepare for the Seder. Thanks to Moshe, I feel more confident that we are conducting the Seder properly."

As Carlos prepared for bed that night, he

could not shake the feeling that danger was all around him. Bella felt it, too. He would have to hurry and put a new escape plan in place.

Chapter Ten

Keeping a Promise

In Amsterdam, Moshe did his best to support his family, but it was difficult. Little Miriam grew so fast that new clothing had to be ordered for her. Due to an unexpectedly cold winter, they burned more firewood than usual. And Yosef, like most growing boys, was always ready for another meal.

One evening, as Moshe slowly unbuttoned his coat after work, he noticed his mother looking worried.

"What is it, Mama?" he asked.

"I know you're trying your best," Mama replied, "but I haven't been able to save anything for Pesach this year. What will we do? I don't want Yosef to leave his Torah studies at such a young age and go to work. Your father would want him to learn for as long as possible."

"I've been thinking about that," Moshe

said, fingering the precious silver buttons. "I do have a plan. Please leave it to me."

Wordlessly, Mama hugged him. Her Moshe was no longer a boy. As the years passed, he had grown tall, and his beard made him look so distinguished. She relied on him completely.

That year, the family did have a lovely Pesach with plenty of matza, good food, and treats for the children. Moshe sat at the Seder table and looked around with satisfaction. The smiling faces of his dear family meant everything to him. Selling the silver buttons from his coat had given him enough to purchase all their needs, and the gift from Carlos was still handsome and warm without them.

"My friend never imagined that he gave me more than a coat," Moshe thought. "Our Pesach this year is thanks to him."

* * *

Time passed, and life settled into a routine. Some weeks there was enough money to pay the bills, and some weeks were difficult. But Moshe and Mama always made sure to put aside something for tzedaka, charity, just as Papa had always done.

One day, a woman from the Jewish community came by to collect for the poor. It was one of those weeks when business was slow. Still, Mama never turned anyone away empty-handed.

"If we can't give money right now," she asked, "would you accept clothing or bedding for the needy?"

"Of course," answered the volunteer. "Any gift is most welcome."

Mama called to Miriam, asking her to bring an old black shawl and a worn blanket from the cedar closet. The young girl grabbed the items, tied them up in a bundle, and handed it to the woman at the door.

"I hope this will keep someone warm and snug for the winter ahead," Mama said.

"Thank you so much," the woman answered. "May Hashem bless you for taking care of the needy."

Later that week, on his way home from work, Moshe felt the first chill of winter. He entered the house, glad that a good fire was blazing.

"Good evening, Mama! I should have worn my coat today. It's starting to feel like winter."

"I'll air it out by the fire, so it will be ready for tomorrow," she answered. "How quickly time passes!"

Mama poured Moshe a cup of hot tea before going back to the cedar closet. She reached in for the coat, pushing other garments out of the way. Puzzled, Mama looked under a pile of winter blankets. The coat wasn't there, but her old black shawl was!

With a sinking feeling, Mama called Miriam aside.

"Miriam, dear child, this was the shawl

I'd intended for the poor. What exactly did you put in that bundle the other day?"

Miriam bit her lip. "I just reached in and pulled out the quilt and something black. The shades were drawn, but it felt like a warm shawl... Have I done something wrong?"

"No, no," Mama answered. But she was more worried than she was willing to admit. Moshe's job had him outdoors, going back and forth with important documents in all types of weather. He needed that coat!

Haltingly, Mama told Moshe about the mistaken donation. Moshe grew pale and thoughtful.

"I'm so sorry, Moshe," said Miriam. "I just didn't realize."

Moshe smiled at her. "I know. It was a mistake. Where is the shawl for the poor?"

Miriam held it out, and Moshe took it with him as he left the house, walking briskly to the shelter for the needy. He entered and noticed a woman who was sorting piles of donated clothing. Respectfully, he explained to her what had happened, and asked for permission to look for his coat.

"Here is the shawl that my mother intended to give to the poor."

The woman nodded and pointed to the recently donated clothing.

Moshe held his breath as he looked through one pile after another. He wondered if he would ever find the coat when it was tangled with so many other garments. What if someone already took it? A thick, expensive coat like that would be the first one chosen.

Moshe tried to calm down. "This coat means so much to me," he thought, "but people are more important than things."

As Moshe reached the bottom of another pile of old coats, he felt the soft wool of a very fine garment, and he held it up to the light. "Can this be my coat from Carlos? Yes! This is it!"

He sat down and gave a sigh of relief.

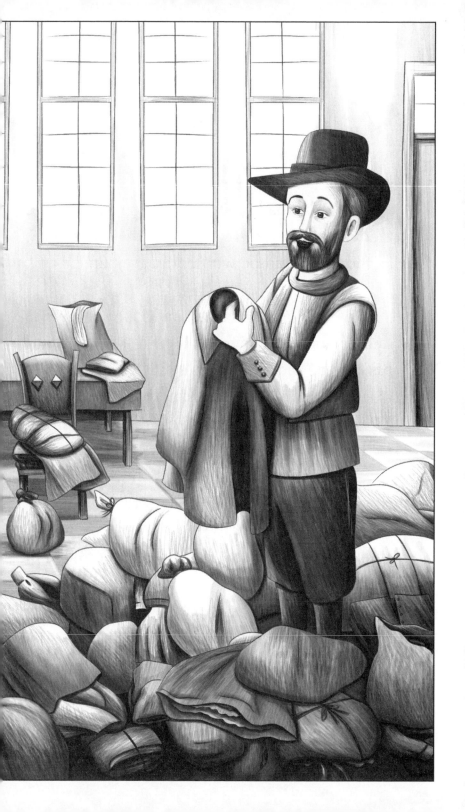

"Thank Hashem I have found my coat, which I need for the winter ahead. More importantly, I'm glad that I can keep my word to a dear friend."

Moshe made sure to leave some additional tzedaka before he left, clutching the coat tightly, as though afraid he would lose it again.

* * *

A few months later, as Moshe set out to deliver some packages, he spied a neighbor of his outside Meneer Jacobs's office.

"Good morning, Meneer van der Markt," Moshe greeted the older man. "What brings you to this part of town?"

"My own business has been taken over by a competitor. I've been looking for work," he answered. From the downcast look on his face, it was easy to tell that his neighbor had not been successful. Moshe felt sorry for this kind and honest man who seemed so discouraged. He shifted the large stack of documents and packages in his arms, wondering what he could do to help. Suddenly, he had an idea.

"I know it's not much," Moshe began, "but would you agree to deliver some sample materials to a warehouse at the edge of the city? I have important documents that I must handle myself, but delivering these packages would at least provide some support for your family."

The two shook hands, and Moshe looked thoughtful as he made his way to his own destination. Why couldn't he start a delivery business and employ honest people to work under him? Every warehouse and office in the city sent out various materials and documents all day long, and some were sensitive and important. This might be a way to provide for his family and help others, too!

If things went well, he could work fewer hours and have more time to study Torah. Imagine if he could buy back their large family home! Imagine if he could give large sums to tzedaka like Papa had done! He'd always admired the van der Markt family... Imagine if he could make his neighbor a partner!

As Moshe went through his day, he couldn't stop dreaming and thinking about a brighter future.

Chapter Eleven
Full Circle

Moshe lost no time in implementing his plan. He and his neighbor started the business as partners and expanded over time. Soon there was enough for the two families to live comfortably, and for the two men to spend only half a day working and the other half learning Torah together.

Moshe never did make a huge fortune, but there was enough to put aside something for the day when Miriam would marry, and enough to keep Yosef from leaving his studies. Moshe never did move his family back to the large home they'd once owned, but his heart was full of happiness that he and his family were living a life that would have made Papa proud.

After a few years passed, Meneer van der Markt proposed that Moshe become his son-in-law, and both families rejoiced. At first, Moshe and his bride, Shifra, lived on the uppermost floor of her family home. There, they welcomed the birth of their first son. In time, they purchased a home nearby and prepared to move.

There was only one topic that always weighed heavily on Moshe's heart. As he explained to his wife, he could never stop wondering about the fate of his friend Carlos Romanus, and what might have happened to his family.

* * *

It was a hot day at the end of summer when Moshe hired a wagon and driver to cart their belongings to their new home. Trip after trip in the blazing sunshine, and soon the new house was full of packages and bundles. Shifra stood at the doorway, holding the baby and instructing the driver and the worker about where to put heavy trunks, furniture, and cooking utensils.

"This wooden chest of drawers goes in the back room, and that smaller one goes in the little room off the kitchen." Shifra fanned her face with her white lace handkerchief. "It is really hot today, and I will be happy when everything is safely in place."

By afternoon, they made the final trip to the new house, and Moshe paid the wagon driver for his work. "You have worked hard all day helping my family, and finally, we are finished! Thank you." Moshe sat down on a chair and sighed.

"There's still more to be done," said Shifra. "I wanted to unpack and organize everything." She lifted the lid of the trunk, and they gazed down at their winter garments.

"It's too hot to handle these heavy woolen blankets, shawls, and coats," said Moshe. "Let's leave this job for a cooler day. I'll just take out my coat and hang it up so it won't wrinkle."

Moshe reached in for the coat, prepared to leave the rest of the items in the trunk. He had put the coat on the very top, but somehow, it was missing. Everything inside had been neatly folded, but now it was all in a jumble. Moshe bent down and lifted a few items out of the way, but his coat was nowhere to be found. Trying not to panic, he emptied all the blankets, shawls, and heavy garments onto the nearest bench. Where was the coat?

Shifra joined him, and they searched through other bundles in other rooms. They looked in every corner of the new house, but it soon became obvious that the overcoat from Carlos Romanus was missing!

"Do you think that the wagon driver took it for himself?" Moshe did not want to believe the worst of anyone, but what else could have happened?

"Perhaps we forgot it at my parents' house," Shifra suggested. "It was quite busy this morning, and maybe your coat was left behind by mistake."

Moshe shook his head. "I am sure that I put it in the trunk with my own two hands. You know how much it means to me."

Shifra knew. They both felt that this exciting move and this special day were under the shadow of the missing coat.

It was after dark when they heard a knock

at the door. Wearily, Moshe went to answer it. To his surprise, there stood the wagon driver.

"Sorry to come so late," he said. "After I went back to stable the horses for the night, I found this in the back of my wagon. It must have fallen out of a trunk during your move."

He held up the precious coat, and Moshe smiled with delight and relief.

"Thank you for returning this so promptly! Such honesty deserves a reward."

Moshe gave the driver a nice sum for returning the coat, and happily hung it up in his new home. The treasured woolen coat from Carlos Romanus was safe for now.

* * *

As time went by, travelers from Spain brought news of terror and despair. The Inquisition kept its powerful hold on Spain, and that spelled disaster for the hidden Jews. Businessmen who had traveled through Spain told frightening stories that Moshe tried to keep from the ears of his wife and his growing family. By now, the couple had two sons and a baby girl.

One particular morning, Moshe heard a tale that brought back memories of his Spanish adventure. A man named Daniel, who used to live in Spain, told everyone there about his narrow escape from the cruelty of the Inquisition.

"You can't imagine how careful we were, but still a neighbor betrayed us. She noticed that my mother changed the bed linen on Friday, and set the table with a white cloth for our Friday evening meal. These simple actions caused an inquiry, and we were forced to flee in the middle of the night with only the clothes on our backs. We were fortunate to escape."

Moshe turned to him. "Have you ever heard of a man named Carlos Romanus? Do you know anything about him?"

Daniel nodded. "He is a wealthy nobleman who owned a vast estate with famous vineyards. Why do you ask?"

Moshe paused. "I had an opportunity to

import some wine, and I wondered if this man was honest."

"I don't know," answered Daniel. "But I also heard that he lost his fortune somehow, and was no longer in the wine business. My information is not recent, so I really have no idea."

Moshe didn't say more. Even now, so many years later and at such a distance, the danger to Carlos and his family was still very real.

Not a day passed that Moshe did not offer a special prayer for the safety of his friend in Spain. During the winter months, he still wore the coat that Carlos had given him. He laughed when he recalled how the coat had been rescued two times – first from the town tzedaka collection and more recently, from the moving day mistake. But he couldn't rescue it from the passage of time.

Shifra brought up the subject one evening when Moshe returned from work.

"Moshe, I know that this coat is very

special to you, but I have patched the lining and sewn new trimming onto the sleeves more than once. There's nothing more I can do if the sleeves fray again."

Moshe looked down. He thought he saw a moth hole on the collar, and the wool was rubbed thin in the back.

"You are right, Shifra," he said, ruefully. "My coat definitely looks worn out, and it is not as comfortable as it used to be where the lining has been patched. I will store it in our room and place an order for a new coat this fall. There is nothing I can do for Carlos and his family, but I will certainly never throw that coat away. I gave him my word."

As he placed the coat securely in an old trunk, Moshe's thoughts turned to the friend he had made so many years ago. "Will I ever see Carlos Romanus again?"

* * *

One winter evening, Moshe and Shifra sat

in their parlor, as a steady, icy rain fell outside. The children were asleep, and the couple was spending a quiet evening relaxing in front of the fire. Shifra was knitting a fluffy wool sweater for their young daughter, and Moshe was content with his book. The wind howled outside, and the sound of raindrops hitting the windows made so much noise that it took a few moments for the couple to hear someone knocking at the front door.

"Moshe," Shifra said, "who could be at our door at this late hour and in such a dreadful storm?"

Moshe jumped to his feet. "Anyone out on a night like this must urgently need help." He made his way to the entry hall and unlatched the front door. An elderly man was standing there, soaked to the skin, shivering in his thin cloak.

"Please, could you spare a bit of food or some money?" asked the beggar. "My family and I are newcomers here."

Moshe and Shifra invited the stranger into their home where it was warm and dry. The poor man's face showed how grateful he was for a minute or two out of the rain. Shifra pretended not to notice how much dripping water was now forming puddles in her spotless hallway. She hurried into the kitchen to prepare some hot food to share with their visitor.

"Thank you so much for your kindness," the beggar said softly. "My family and I have been without food for two days, and anything you offer us would be a mitzva indeed."

Moshe sat with their visitor, keeping him company and making conversation. "My wife will pack some food for your family, but do you need a place to stay?"

"No thank you, kind sir, we have an adequate place to stay in the communal house, but there is not enough food for everyone there. We have spent the past several months wandering around trying to find a place to settle."

Moshe felt drawn to this stranger and wanted to help him. "Where have you come from?"

The stranger sighed. "My family and I were forced to leave Spain, and that is why we are wandering about."

"Spain? Officially, there are no Jews in Spain."

"You are right, of course," the stranger replied. "No Jews dare live openly in Spain, but my family and I lived as hidden Jews for generations until we were discovered and forced to run for our lives!"

Moshe leaned forward. "How did they discover your secret?"

The stranger shook his head. "It was unbelievable. For generations, my family and I were good Spanish citizens, successful and generous. Everything was undone by a kitchen servant who testified that we never added cream or milk to meat recipes, and that my wife prepared a hot dish on Friday that we ate the next afternoon. Imagine being betrayed by such simple actions!"

Moshe was so moved by this amazing sacrifice for Torah and mitzvot that he couldn't speak.

The man continued in a soft voice. "We lived in a beautiful village in coastal Spain, in a large house on the hillside. Our home was the envy of everyone in town, and if they could see me now, they would not believe that I am the same man. But in truth, I am not the same man. I am happier than I've ever been, now that I can live openly as a Jew."

Moshe studied the beggar's face. The old man seemed so familiar, though his voice was hoarse and his face deeply lined and weathered. It was impossible. It couldn't be, but Moshe was determined to find out. He spoke slowly, trying to find the words.

"I once found myself in Spain, and I met

a hidden Jew there, many years ago. He, too, lived in a large house on a hillside and achieved much success in business. But he hated that life of danger and secrecy. He was determined to leave Spain with his wife and children. His name was Carlos Romanus..."

The stranger grew pale and gasped. "Moshe, Moshe, my dearest friend! Hashem has led me straight to you after all my suffering and wandering!"

The two long-lost friends embraced and cried together.

"Moshe, I didn't recognize you after all these years... and here you are, grown and married! Thank Hashem, I chose to walk down your street and knock on your door! I cannot believe that after all these years I found you, and that you still remember my family and me."

"Remember you?" Shifra wiped her eyes and laughed. "Señor Romanus, not a day goes by without my husband talking about you and

your family. You have been in our prayers since my husband returned home all those years ago."

Moshe turned to his wife, his face shining with excitement. "Shifra, I will go with Carlos to fetch his wife and children. I won't rest a moment until they are all here under our roof for the night."

The older man's thin cloak was still dripping wet, so Moshe brought out the coat he had stored away. "Here, my friend. I kept this all through the years of our separation, just as you requested. This coat kept me warm and dry as I went out in the world to earn my living. It reminded me of you, and it inspired me to keep my Jewish heritage with joy. Now, I present it back to you as a gift. It's well-worn and well-loved, but it will keep you warm tonight. Tomorrow, you must allow me to order new garments and coats for your entire family."

Carlos swayed on his feet, and Moshe quickly brought a chair. "What is it? Are you ill?"

Carlos gasped weakly, "The coat! That's the

coat! After all this time, I'd forgotten. Give it to me... please give it to me!"

Moshe was puzzled, but he placed the coat in Carlos's hands. The older man fumbled with the garment, turning it, clutching it, and ripping the hem from edge to edge. Shifra and Moshe looked at each other in concern. Had the shock affected his mind?

In a stronger voice, Carlos said, "Look! Look what I hid inside the coat all those years ago!"

With trembling hands, he unrolled the hem to reveal a long row of diamonds, sparkling in the firelight.

Moshe gasped and stared at the beautiful jewels.

"Why, these are worth a fortune! My dear, dear friend, you will have enough to support your family and start your new life!"

Once again, the two men embraced and cried with joy.

"My dearest Moshe, when we met in

Spain, it didn't take long for me to realize that I could trust you. When we parted, I knew that you would safeguard the coat and keep your word to me. A good friend is worth more than diamonds!"

Moshe was overcome. His adventure with Carlos Romanus was filled with hidden miracles, now clear for all to see. Moshe shook his head in amazement.

"Hashem has indeed given me the opportunity to repay you for your kindness and hospitality all those years ago. Now let us hurry. I cannot wait to welcome your family into my home tonight."

Historical Note

The Secret of Carlos Romanus takes place during one of the cruelest periods in Jewish history. **The Spanish Inquisition** was established in 1478 by Ferdinand and Isabella, the rulers of Spain. Jews were banished a few years later in 1492, when they were ordered to convert or leave the country.

Some of the wealthiest Jews were forced to convert and not permitted to leave. Some Jews converted to save their lives, but kept mitzvot in secret. These converts, or conversos, were sometimes called **marranos** (Spanish for "pig" and a very insulting term) and were watched closely to see if they really believed in the church's teachings or not.

Anyone who was accused of being disloyal to the church was ordered to appear in front of an inquisition tribunal, which was like a trial. The judge was called the **Inquisitor**. But these trials were different from regular court cases – and very unfair in many ways.

All the money and property belonging to an accused secret Jew would be taken by the government to pay for the trial and his stay in prison. The person would be forced to testify, and he didn't get a lawyer or any help at all. If he refused to testify, the Inquisitor took this refusal as proof of his guilt. Anybody could give evidence against him, including criminals... or even his own wife and children! Most of the time, he wouldn't be told who his accusers were.

The accused usually didn't have any witnesses testify for him, because they would automatically be suspected of being disloyal to the church themselves. The accused wasn't always immediately told what the charges were against him, so it was impossible to defend himself.

Even simple household practices noticed by servants or nosy neighbors could put an entire family in danger. They could be found guilty for any Jewish behaviors like:

"...changing into clean personal linen on (Shabbat) and wearing better clothes than on other days; preparing on Fridays the food for (Shabbat), in stewing pans on a small fire; who do not work on Friday evenings and (Shabbat) as on other days; who kindle lights in clean lamps with new wicks on Friday evening; place clean linen on the beds and clean napkins on the table; celebrate the festival of the unleavened bread, eat unleavened bread and celery and bitter herbs... who do not wish to eat salt pork, hares, rabbits, snails, or fish that have not scales..."

(Edict of Faith, issued in Valencia in 1519 by Inquisitor Andres de Palacio*)

Like the fictional Carlos Romanus and his family, many secret Jews had little knowledge of Judaism after several generations had passed. Still, they exhibited great self-sacrifice for the mitzvot they did cherish and keep. To this day, it is inspiring to read accounts of these brave men and women who suffered so much for their fierce desire to remain loyal Jews.

*Cecil Roth, *The Spanish Inquisition*, (New York: W. W. Norton & Company, 1964) 77/79